Little Princess

THIS BOOK BELONGS TO

_____

To Arie and Nell

Ⓐ

This paperback edition first published in 2019 by Andersen Press Ltd.
First published in Great Britain in 2018 by
Andersen Press Ltd., 20 Vauxhall Bridge Road, London SW1V 2SA.
Copyright © Tony Ross, 2018.
The rights of Tony Ross to be identified as the author and illustrator of this work
have been asserted by him in accordance with the Copyright, Designs and Patents Act, 1988.
All rights reserved. Colour separated in Switzerland by Photolitho AG, Zürich.
Printed and bound in Malaysia.

1   3   5   7   9   10   8   6   4   2

British Library Cataloguing in Publication Data available.

ISBN 978 1 78344 755 8

I Want My Dad!

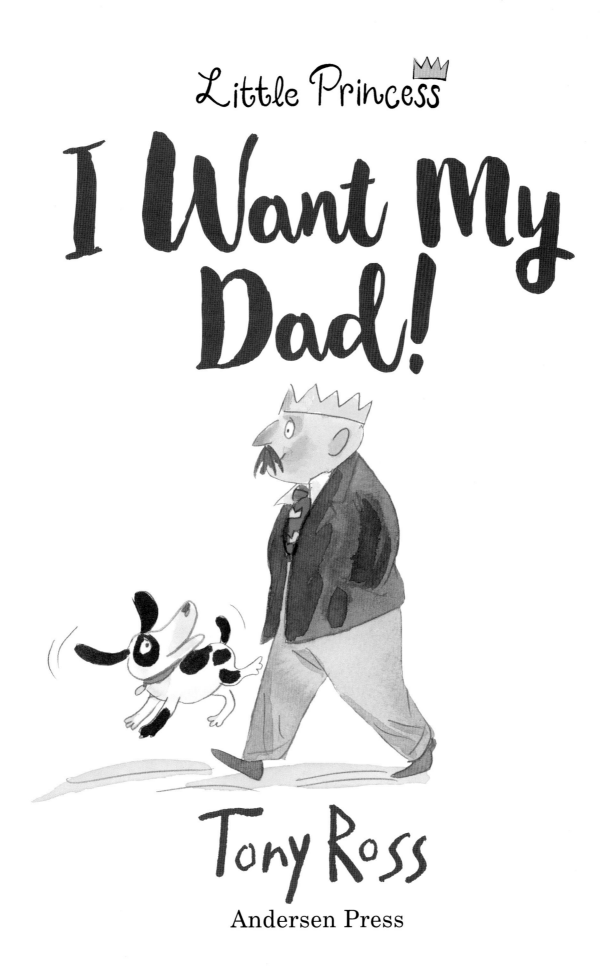

Tony Ross

Andersen Press

The Little Princess was proud of her dad, the King.
He was taller than all the other dads.

Except when the other dads stood up.
Then, the Little Princess became a bit jealous.

The Cook was taller than the Little Princess's dad,
especially with his hat on, and he baked his son
the most wonderful cakes.

Even the dog would not eat the famous
burned-black cakes that her dad baked.

The General taught his son to ride a pony.

But whenever her dad went near animals (even her mouse)
they made him sneeze.

The Admiral taught his daughter to swim.

But the King needed armbands in the bath –
he never swam, he just sank like a stone.

The Gardener took his twins on adventure
walks in the forest.

The King got lost on his way to bed.

"I wish my dad was as much fun as other dads!"
the Little Princess wailed to the Maid.

"I wish he could teach me to ride and cook and swim,
and take me on adventure walks. He's useless."

"I can teach you all of those things!" said the Maid.

So, the Maid taught her to trot on her pony.
But the Little Princess fell off and bumped her head.

Then the Maid showed her how to make a cake.
But the Little Princess's cake was so hard, it hurt her teeth.

Then the Maid taught her how to swim.
But the Little Princess swallowed lots of horrible water.

Then the Maid took her for an adventure walk in the woods.
But the Little Princess got them lost, so they missed their tea.

The Little Princess felt cold, she felt wet, her teeth hurt, her head-bump hurt, and she was very, very hungry.

She also felt that she couldn't do anything properly.
In fact, she felt quite miserable.

Just then, the King walked by with the dog.

"I WANT MY DAD!" the Little Princess squealed,
rushing up to him. "Dad, I'm useless."

"What can you mean?" said the King, hugging his daughter.
"When I heard about you doing all of those exciting things…"

"I felt so PROUD!"